Peace Begins with You

The Sierra Club, founded in 1892 by John Muir, has devoted itself to the study and protection of the earth's scenic and ecological resources — mountains, wetlands, woodlands, wild shores and rivers, deserts and plains. The publishing program of the Sierra Club offers books to the public as a nonprofit educational service in the hope that they may enlarge the public's understanding of the Club's basic concerns. The Sierra Club has some sixty chapters in the United States and in Canada. For information about how you may participate in its programs to preserve wilderness and the quality of life, please address inquiries to Sierra Club, 85 Second Street, San Francisco, CA 94105

Text copyright © 1989 by Katherine Scholes
Illustrations copyright © 1989 by Robert Ingpen

First U.S. Paperback Edition: May 1994

First published in Australia by Michelle Anderson Publishing Pty Ltd., Melbourne

Library of Congress Cataloging-in-Publication Data
Scholes, Katherine.
  [Peacetimes]
  Peace begins with you/Katherine Scholes; illustrated by Robert Ingpen. — 1st U.S. ed.
    p. cm.
  Originally published: Peacetimes. Australia: Michelle Anderson Publishing Pty Ltd, © 1989
  Summary: Explains, in simple terms, the concept of peace, why conflicts occur, how they can be resolved in positive ways, and how to protect peace.
  ISBN 978-0-316-77440-6 (pb)
  1. Peace — Juvenile literature. [1. Peace.] I. Ingpen, Robert R., ill. II. Title.
JX1963.S255   1990
303.6'6 — dc20   90-33752

Sierra Club Books/Little, Brown children's books are published by Little, Brown and Company (Inc.) in association with Sierra Club Books.

20 19 18 17 16 15 14

Printed in Thailand

Peace Begins with You

Katherine Scholes • Illustrated by Robert Ingpen

Sierra Club Books
San Francisco

LITTLE, BROWN AND COMPANY
New York · Boston

Peace
can feel warm, bright, and strong—
or calm, cool, and gentle.

It can be found in a place that is busy and loud—
and be missing in the calmest, quietest place on earth.

Peace means different things to different people,
in different places, at different times in their lives.

So . . .
What is peace?
Where does it come from?
How can you find it?
And how can you keep it?

There are some things you need just to stay alive:
food, water, a place to live,
clothes to keep warm,
help when you are ill or injured . . .

Peace is having the things you need.

Then there are things that you want,
to help make life good.

Small things . . .
like a cup of hot chocolate on a winter evening,
or a walk along an empty beach,
or a special place to be alone with your friends.

And big things . . .
like not being afraid,
like having the chance to study and learn,
like knowing you are loved by family or friends.

Peace is being able to have,
or to hope for and work for,
at least some of the things you want.

Everybody is different.
They want and need different things, in different places,
at different times in their lives.

Peace is being allowed to be different—
and letting others be different from you.

Because people are different,
their needs or wants don't always fit easily together,
in the same place, at the same time.

And even when people are not very different
there can be problems.
They may want to have or use the same thing
at the same time.
Or there may not be enough of something
that everybody wants
to go around.

Living with others means you can't always have
what you need or want
when, where, or exactly how you would like it.
It means that sometimes your feeling of peace
will be interrupted—
in a small way, or in a big way.

Some people have tried living all by themselves,
so that their peace would be complete.
But often it doesn't work.
They feel lonely—
and loneliness is not a peaceful feeling.

So what can be done when people's needs or wants
don't seem to fit together?

There can be arguments, angry words, silences—
or even fighting.
It can go on for a long time, or a short time,
until one side wins, and the other loses—
until one gets what they want or need,
and the other gives up.

When this happens peace is interrupted.

But something completely different can happen.
There can be another kind of argument—
one where both sides explain what they need or want,
and why,
where they listen to one another,
where they work together to solve the problem
so that both sides can have what they need or want—
or at least some of it . . .

Sometimes other people, outside the problem,
can help this to happen.
They can say if someone is being unfair,
or breaking the rules of the argument.

They can suggest ways of solving the problem
so that peace is not interrupted.

And sometimes,
between two different paths that can't be brought together,
a third way can be found—
one that is different from what was first needed or wanted,
but that is good for both sides.

The third way may even be a better way—for everybody!
Conflict can be the beginning
of something new, and good.

But what happens when no third way can be found—
when people have talked, listened, thought . . .
and still,
their needs or wants just can't be fitted together?

There are still choices that can be made.
The two sides could agree to move apart,
so that neither gets what they first wanted.
Or they could make a deal involving other things
they both need or want.

There are always choices that can be made.

Some choices threaten peace.
Some choices protect it.

Every day, people make choices about peace
at home, at school, at work . . .

Their choices affect others as well as themselves.

The same kinds of choices are made
when there are problems between one country and another.
Some choices lead, in the end, to war.

But through people talking, listening,
and working things out together,
peace can be protected.

It's not always easy. It takes two to work together.
But it also takes two to fight.
And often it only takes one to begin the first step
toward a peaceful solution.

Working for peace may be harder than using force.
You may have to be braver and stronger.
You may have to learn new skills,
new ways of thinking and planning.

But when you consider how much pain is caused
by the breaking of peace—
in families, neighborhoods, and countries
all over the world
and all through time—
it has to be worth it.

Peace has to be a better way.

Some people think only about having peace for themselves.
They don't care about what others need or want.
They try to stay inside their own peaceful place
and keep everyone else's problems outside it.

They might get away with this
for a little—or even a long—while.
But in the end, the only hope of lasting peace—
in our homes, our communities,
and all the countries of the world—
is a peace that is real for everyone.

This can only begin to happen
when more people work toward making sure others
have the things they need,
and at least some of the things they want—
when more people work toward making sure
everyone is treated fairly.

All through history, there have been peacemakers—
people who have worked for peace
by trying to make life better for others.
They have worked to have laws changed
and things shared more fairly,
so that everyone—whoever and wherever they are—
can have the chance of a good life.

Being a peacemaker often means saying "No!"
It may mean starting a conflict.
Because if you believe something is wrong, or unfair,
you may have to speak up, and you may have to act.

But there are many different ways to speak and act,
and some are more likely to bring change,
with peace, than others.

Our world is full of change.
Ideas and beliefs change, ways of living change,
the natural world itself changes—
in our lifetimes,
and across whole chapters of history.

And our ideas about what we need,
and especially what we want,
change as well.

To keep up with these changes, we have invented new ways
of finding and using
more and more of what our planet can give us.
Often this causes conflict
between the needs of plants and animals
and the needs or wants of people.

And too often it's people who have their way.

But all living things are part of one giant web of life.
And—in the end—they all depend on one another.

So when we think about the future,
we must think about living in peace with the land.

Caring about problems in the world,
and even having problems of your own,
doesn't mean you can't feel peace anymore.

There is a special kind of peace that lives inside you.
Some people can feel this peace
even when they are in great pain, fear, or danger.

Many different philosophies and religious faiths
teach about this "inside" peace—
and also about making peace in the world.

Peace
is not a gap between times of fighting,
or a space where nothing is happening.

Peace
is something that
lives,
grows,
spreads—
and needs to be looked after.

How to be a peacemaker

Learn about what is happening in the world around you.
Learn about different ways of living and thinking.
Be involved in the decisions being made on your behalf
by parents, teachers, counselors, politicians.

But first of all,
learn about yourself,
about why you think, believe, feel, and act as you do.
Learn how to listen
and how to see things from another point of view.
Learn how to solve problems peacefully in your own life,
because peace begins with you—
in your own backyard.